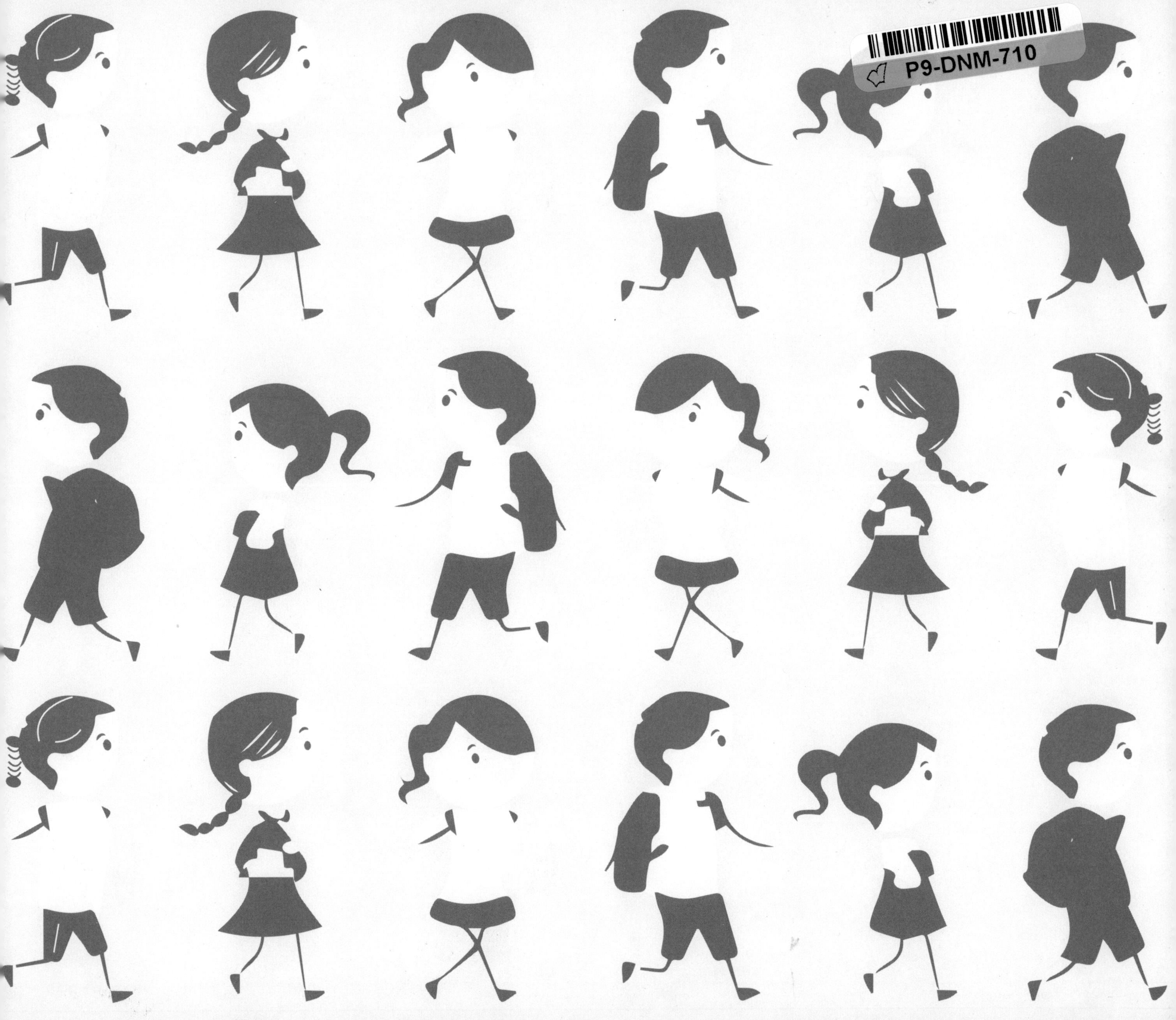

"Fall in Line, Holden!"

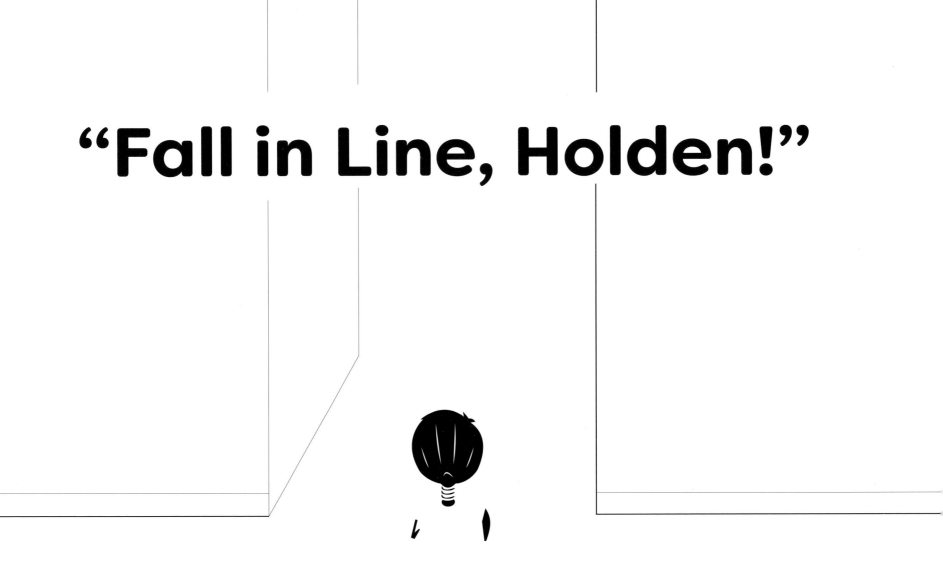

Written and Illustrated By

Daniel W. Vandever

Library of Congress Cataloging-in-Publication Data

Names: Vandever, Daniel W., author, illustrator.
Title: Fall in line, Holden / written and illustrated By Daniel W. Vandever.
Description: First edition. | Flagstaff, Arizona : Salina Bookshelf, Inc.,
[2017] | Summary: At a very strict school in Indigenous Nation, everyone but Holden stays in line until they reach the door at the end of the school day.

Identifiers: LCCN 2017000913 | ISBN 9781893354500 (hardcover : alk. paper)
Subjects: | CYAC: Stories in rhyme. | Schools--Fiction. | Behavior--Fiction. | Indians of North America--Fiction.
Classification: LCC PZ8.3.V3343 Fal 2017 | DDC [E]--dc23 LC record available at https://lccn.loc.gov/2017000913

Edited by LaFrenda Frank
Designed by Corey Begay

Printed in the United States of America

First Printing, First Edition
23 22 21 20 19 18 17 8 7 6 5 4 3 2 1

The paper used in this publication meets the minimum requirements of the American National Standard for Information Sciences — Permanence of Paper for Printed Library Materials, ANSI Z39.48-1984.

Salina Bookshelf, Inc.
Flagstaff, Arizona 86001
www.salinabookshelf.com

To my nieces and nephews,
Thanks for playing with me when I visit.
Never be afraid to fall out of line.

-Uncle Dan

Deep in the heart of Indigenous Nation,
Stood a strict Western school of stern education.
Where everyone obeyed and did what they were told,
And conformity ruled all to fit like a mold.

Until a boy fell out of line...

As class ends
and recess begins,
we all fall in line.

We pass through the halls
with art-covered walls.
We all fall in line.

We march left and then right,
with no end in our sight.
We all fall in line.

CUSTODIAN

We bypass the laughs
of the custodial staff.
We all fall in line.

We move slowly in silence
with no words of defiance.
We all fall in line.

We pass the school's gym
as a battle begins.
We all fall in line.

GYMNASIUM

Our tired minds lag
and our heavy feet drag.
We all fall in line.

We pass the lunch crew
to the smell of mutton stew.
We all fall in line.

We do as we're told
and don't dare to be bold.
We all fall in line.

COMPUTER LAB

In respectable fashion,
we pass the lab's distractions.
We all fall in line.

And though our backs ache;
our spirits never break.
We all fall in line.

MUSIC

Our class rambles on
to the band's rhythmic song.
We all fall in line.

With the playground in sight
and just a glimmer of light,
we all fall in line.

But as we reach the door,
we can't take it anymore.

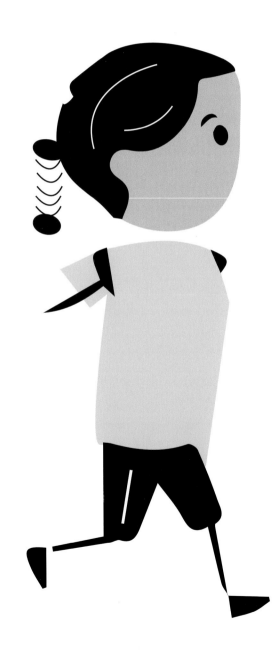

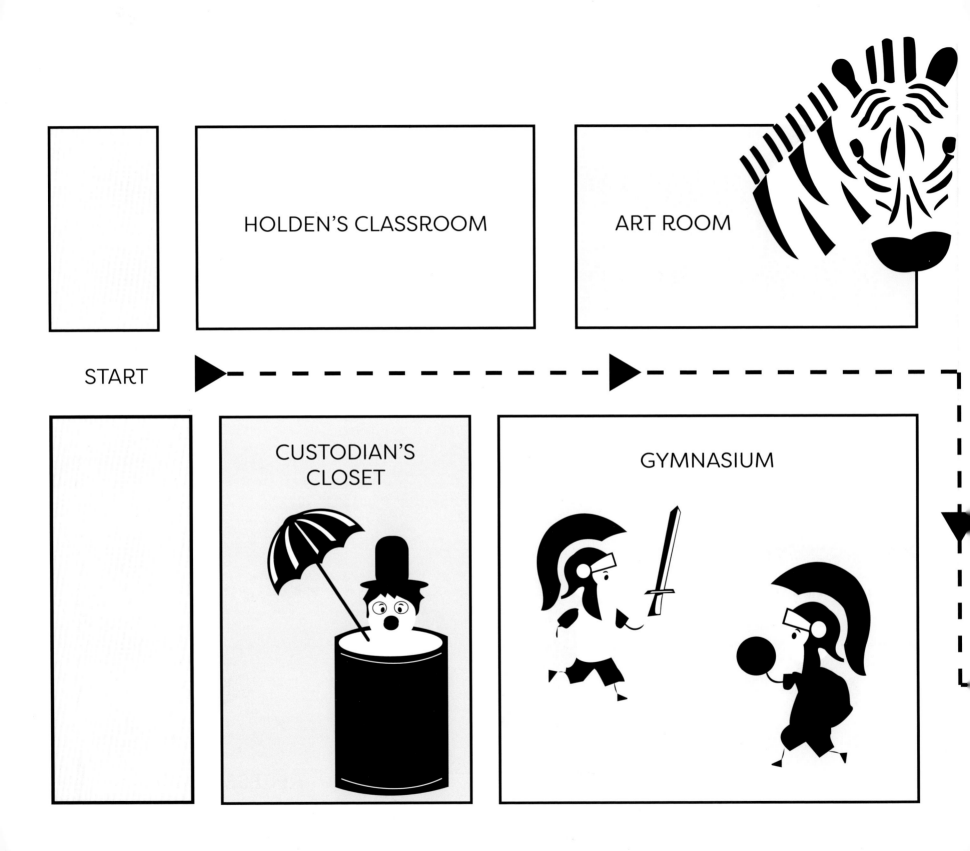

HOLDEN'S CLASSROOM

ART ROOM

START

CUSTODIAN'S CLOSET

GYMNASIUM

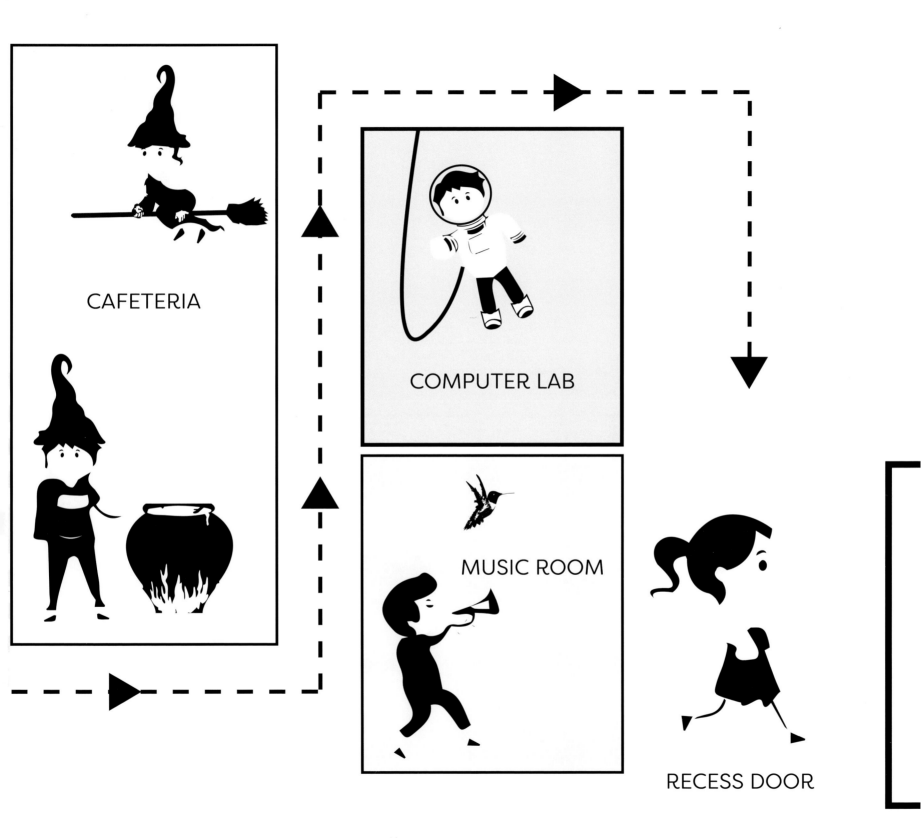

CAFETERIA

COMPUTER LAB

MUSIC ROOM

RECESS DOOR

Author's note

Fall in Line, Holden was written with the intention of promoting creative thinking and originality, but also to begin conversations about a grim period in American history. Boarding school education has many connotations to different people, but to an entire generation of Indigenous people it was a militant term of conformity and an attack on language and culture. Thus, a generation of individuals were detached from their sense of identity resulting in a generational disconnect that has exacerbated the negative social and economic conditions that exist in many Indigenous communities today.

Acknowledgement

Boarding school education has had a profound impact on the loss of culture and identity in many Indigenous communities, resulting in poor economic and social conditions. To all those who survived boarding school education, my father included, thank you for your sacrifices. We are now able to move forward with both Western and traditional knowledge in taking ownership of our future based on the resilience of our past. Ahe'hee shik'é dóó shidiné'e.

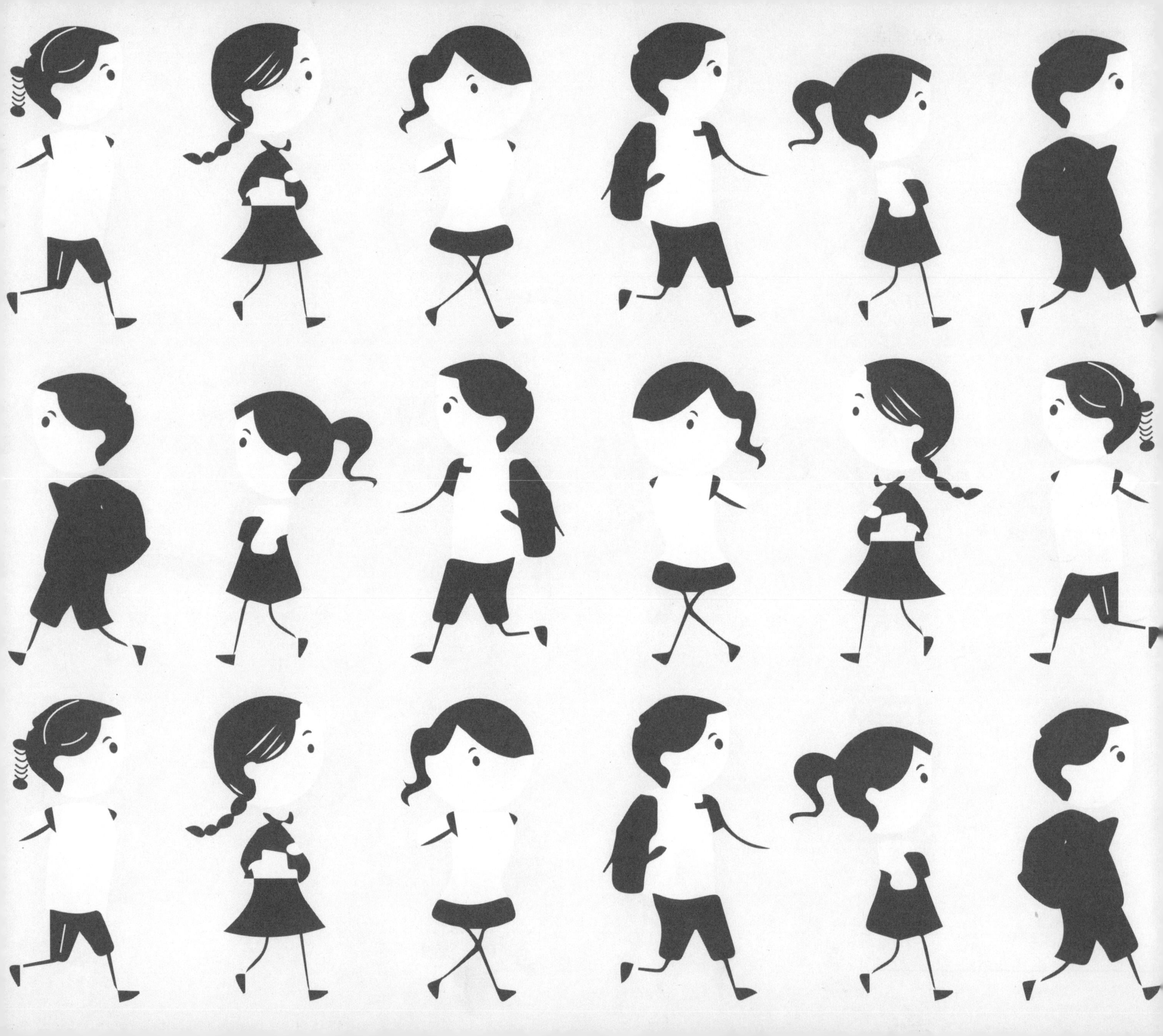

First edition 2017

Library of Congress Catalog Card Number pending
ISBN 978-0-7636-7291-1

17 18 19 20 21 22 CCP 10 9 8 7 6 5 4 3 2 1

Printed in Shenzhen, Guangdong, China

MIX
Paper from
responsible sources
FSC® C008047
FSC
www.fsc.org

This book was typeset in Gotham.
The illustrations were created digitally.

Candlewick Studio
an imprint of Candlewick Press
99 Dover Street
Somerville, Massachusetts 02144

www.candlewickstudio.com

DOUBLE TAKE!
A New Look at Opposites

Susan Hood

illustrated by Jay Fleck

CANDLEWICK STUDIO
an imprint of Candlewick Press

For Emily and Peter, two sides of one heart,
and for all the roads ahead
S. H.

To Suzanne, Audrey, and Owen with love
J. F.

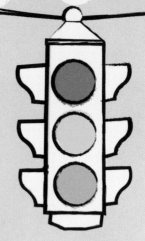

Do you know opposites—
YES or NO?

If I say STOP,
you say GO.

If I say LEFT,

you say RIGHT!

IN?

OUT!

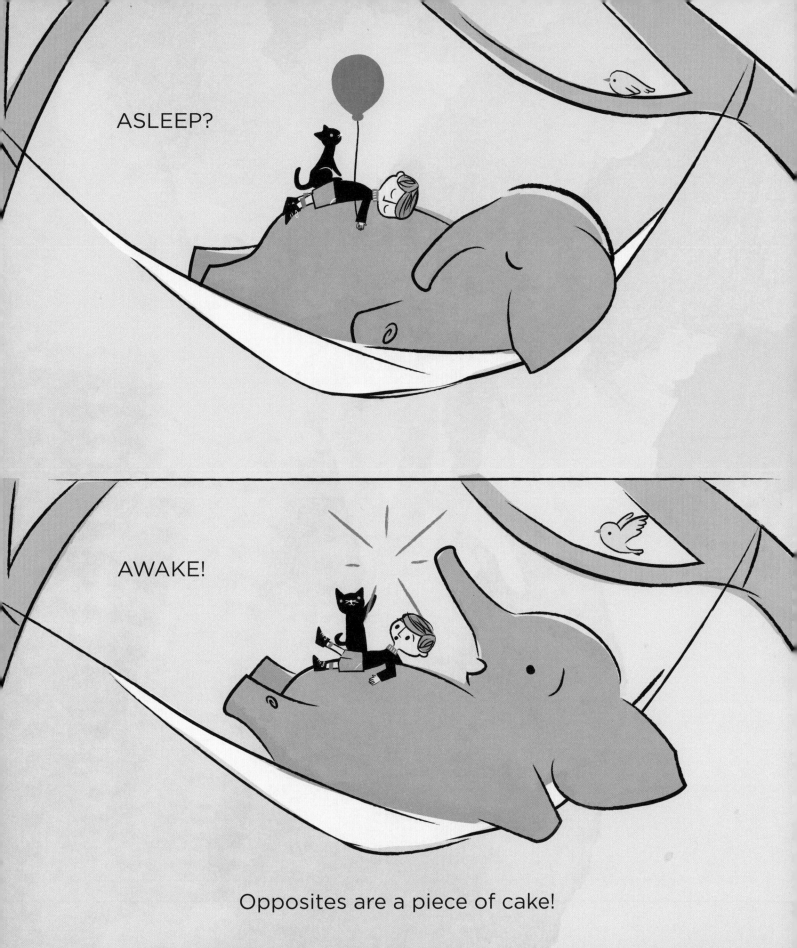

While those pairs are plain

as DAY . . .

and NIGHT,

not every duo is so BLACK and WHITE.

Who knows what is **BIG**

unless there is SMALL?

Does SHORT measure up
except next to TALL?

HIGH might look hazy

until we see LOW.

A racer's called *FAST*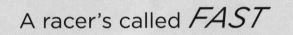

when rivals are S L O W .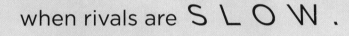

Now just when you think you've mastered that notion, watch relative words set matters in motion.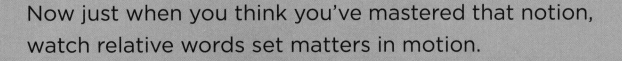

Who's NEAR   and   who's FAR

couldn't be clearer,

but . . .

does
NEAR
become
FAR

when FAR flies in NEARer?

Who's **STRONG**

and who's WEAK
is hardly perplexing.

But **STRONG** can look WEAK
when a **new champ** is flexing!

Point of view (where you are)
can affect what you see.
Go in close. Then back up—
you'll see differently!

These dashes and dots
in a rainbow array . . .

can paint a new picture when you step away!

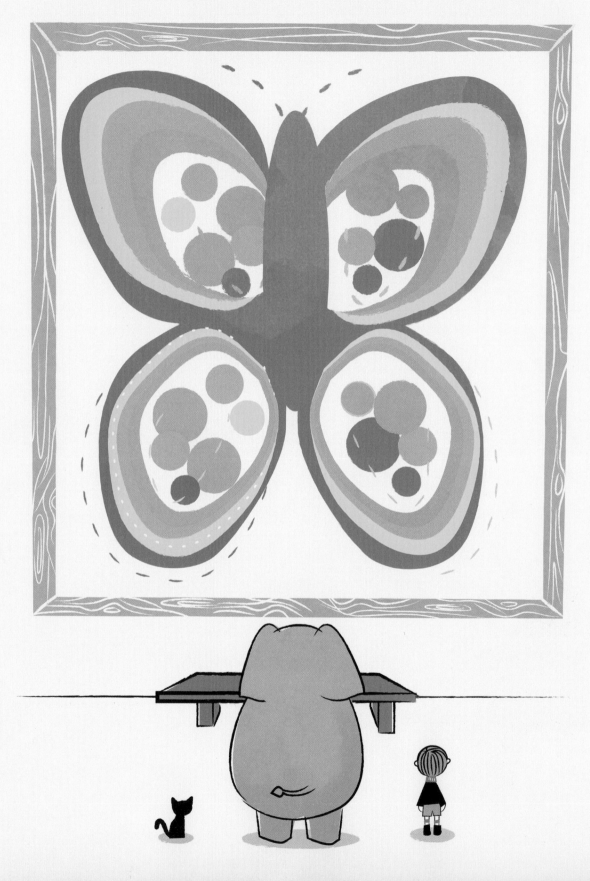

Who is AHEAD
and who is BEHIND . . .

is different for everyone standing in line.

What is ABOVE

and what is BELOW?

The answer depends on who wants to know.

A careless assumption can be a mistake.
Look once, then again;
do a quick double take!

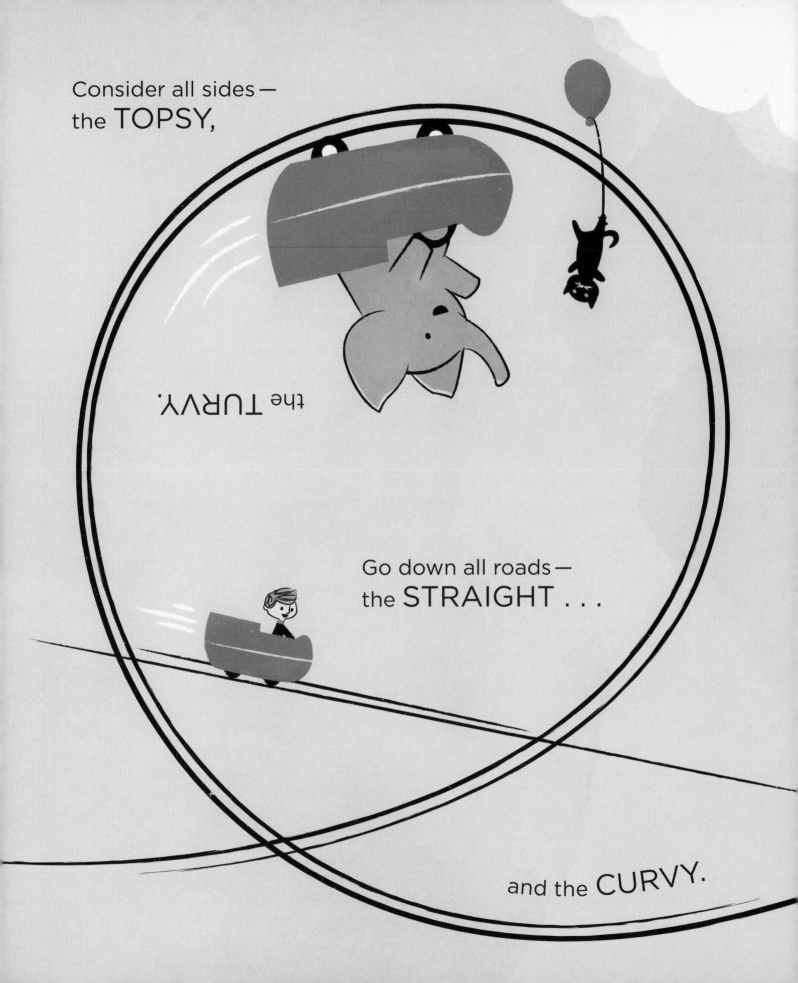

Consider all sides—
the TOPSY,

the TURVY,

Go down all roads—
the STRAIGHT . . .

and the CURVY.

Turn things around! Give them a twist.
FIND a new view
that you might have MISSED!

A brand-new direction, a closer inspection,
might lead to reflection and maybe . . .

perfection.